Howard B. Wigglebottom Learns We Can All Get Along

Howard Binkow   Reverend Ana

David A. Cutting   Mike Ferrin

SCHOLASTIC INC.

Howard Binkow Reverend Ana

THANKS

Our special gratitude to the following people:
Joanne, Sophia and Eric De Graaf, Cindy Herbert, Jacqui Odell, Tori Peterson, Rebecca Rowell, Julia Simpson, Rosemary Underwood, and Suzanne Zottola—their comments made the book much better!

We also give appreciation and gratitude to those volunteers who gave us feedback and the schools that participated in the review process:
Christ Church School, Ft. Lauderdale, Florida; Garden Elementary, Venice, Florida; Greater Summit County Early Learning Center, Akron, Ohio; Holy Child Jesus School, Richmond Hill, New York; and SCOPE Academy, Akron, Ohio.

ISBN 978-0-545-79974-4

Published by Scholastic Inc., 557 Broadway, New York, NY 10012, by arrangement with We Do Listen Foundation.

12 11 10 9 8 7 6 5 4 3 2 1 14 15 16 17 18 19/0

Printed in the U.S.A. 40

First Scholastic printing, September 2014

Illustration by David A. Cutting and Mike Ferrin
Book design by Jane Darroch Riley

This book belongs to

____

"Howard B. Wigglebottom, why are you so sad today?" asked Grandma.

"Ali is having a picnic party and I'm not invited," cried Howard. "She said I am no fun."

“Any idea why Ali would say that?” Grandma wanted to know.

“Maybe because I want my friends to cheer for my team instead of the one they like?” answered Howard. “We end up fighting.”

"Or can it be because I hide the ball when I want us to play video games instead?" Howard wondered. "Then, we all fight."

“Nope,” he said, pausing. “I think it’s because I cut in line at lunch. There’s always a fight when I do that.”

“Wait! I know! I get mad if I don’t get to be right. Ali says I pick a fight when I am not right,” said Howard.

“So, you pick or cause fights all the time! No wonder you are not invited,” Grandma told him.

“But Granny, I so want to go to this party! How about if I disguise myself as a new kid on the block and just show up?”

“Or maybe I can be disguised as someone else,” suggested Howard.
“Please help! How can I go to the party?”

“How about,” said Grandma with a big smile, “if you go disguised as someone who knows how to get along with your friends?”

"Howard, my dear, it sounds like you need to learn important lessons before you can be invited anywhere!" Grandma exclaimed.

“Would I be able to go to the party if I learned the lessons right away?” Howard was interested.

“I’m not sure you have enough time, Howard,” Grandma replied. “Without practicing, it’s too hard to learn a new way of doing things, but let’s try.”

“Would you like your big brother telling you which team you can root for?” asked Grandma.

“No, Granny, I wouldn’t,” Howard said. “I like to pick my own teams. So, I should not tell my friends whom to root for, right?”

“Right!” Grandma cheered. “Everyone needs to have a say.”

MY
WAY
MY
TEAM

“How would you like your little sister telling you what to play with?” Grandma asked next.

“No way!” answered Howard. “So, I should not make my friends always play what I want to play?”

"Right!" cheered Grandma again. "Everyone needs to have a say."

"How would you like someone cutting in line in front of you?
You would scream and shove and get very angry, right?" asked Grandma.

"Oh, yes! I know, Granny, I know! I can't cut in line anymore. I shouldn't do to my friends what I wouldn't like my friends to do to me, right?" Howard asked.

"Right you are! To get along with your friends, you can't always have your way. Everyone needs to have a say and a turn!" explained Grandma.

"Howard," Grandma continued, "we all want to be right. When we are right, we feel special. The trick is to share being right. Let your friends be right, too!"

"Yes, I've got it!" said Howard. "I will remember from now on: everyone gets the chance to be right, have a say, and have a turn!"

WE All Get To Be Right

As soon as he could, Howard talked to Ali: “Please forgive me. I learned my lesson about how to get along with friends. PLEASE let me go to the party, even though I haven’t had much time to practice.”

Howard promised everyone would have a chance to be right, have a turn, and have a say. And so they did, and they all had a grand time at the party.

Howard B. Wigglebottom Learns We Can All Get Along

Suggestions for Lessons and Reflections

To get along with our friends and loved ones means we are nice, kind, and respectful to them whenever we can be.

When we get along with others, we feel good and life is easy.

Is it easy to get along with everyone?

No. Some people make it very hard for us to get along with them.

Are you easy to get along with? Are your friends easy to get along with?

Did Howard know how to get along with his friends?

No, he didn't. His friends thought he was no fun until his grandma taught him the rules to get along.

★ RULE #1: EVERYONE NEEDS TO HAVE A SAY

To have a say means we can say what we think, want, and feel and others will not get mad at or make fun of us. When we have a say, we feel respected and loved.

Did Howard let his friends have a say at the beginning of the story?

No, he didn't. By hiding the ball, he wanted to make his friends play what he wanted to play. And by making his friends root for his team only, Howard wanted them to think the way he did.

What happened when Howard didn't let his friends have a say? He and his friends fought and got in trouble.

If you don't want to get in trouble all the time, practice letting your friends have a say. Let them play and think what they want, especially if it's different than what you want to play and what you think.

★ RULE #2: EVERYONE NEEDS TO HAVE A TURN

To have a turn means to have a fair chance to do something you want.

When we let our friends have a turn, we don't cut in line and we share our toys and other things.

Did Howard let his friends have a turn?

No, he didn't. He always cut in line. What happened when he did that? Howard and his friends fought and got in trouble.

Don't get in trouble. Let your friends have their turn to play, to eat, to speak, to sit at the place where everyone wants to sit, and so on.

★ RULE #3: EVERYONE GETS TO BE RIGHT

To be right about something means what we think and say is true and better than what others think or say. Most of us feel very good when we are right about things.

Some of us get very upset if we don't get to be right all the time.

Do you like to be right about things?

How do you feel when you are wrong?

Did Howard let his friends be right at the beginning of the story? No, he didn't. He picked a fight and got in trouble when he didn't get to be right.

Don't fight with your friends and get in trouble. Practice letting your friends be right, too! Sharing being right is a sure way to get along with everyone!

★ RULE #4: APOLOGIZE

Respecting others means to let them have a say and a turn and to be right. When we fail to respect our friends, we must apologize to them right away. We have to let them know we didn't mean to make them feel bad. If we want our friends to respect us, always treat them the way we want to be treated, and we should ONLY use words that make them feel good, not bad.

Remember, for us to be happy and healthy, we need to get along with others and treat everyone the way we like to be treated: with kindness and respect!

WEB SITE

Visit www.wedolisten.org:

• Enjoy free animated books, games, and songs.

• Print lessons and posters from the books, and contact us.